AVINASHYA

THE INDESTRUCTIBLE

SRAVAN VEMULA

Contents

Prologue v

1. Chapter Ekam 1
2. Chapter Dve 8
3. Chapter Treeni 11
4. Chapter Chatvaari 16
5. Chapter Pancha 22
6. Chapter Shat 26
7. Chapter Sapta 31
8. Chapter Ashta 36
9. Chapter Nava 46
10. Chapter Dasha 54
11. Chapter Ekaadasha 60
12. Chapter Dvaadasha 66
13. Chapter Trayodasha 76
14. Chapter Chaturdasha 81

Prologue

Legend says, before the universe that we know existed, Mother and Father were the only two celestial beings. Father was destroyed by Mother during a heated battle between the two celestials. Father's spine was separated and was stuck to the floor in the Throne room. Mother later created angels and the angels were then assigned different responsibilities.

Mother had been asleep for many millenniums. Even though she is asleep, she kept an eye on EVERYTHING.

Kala, Angel of time and fate, foresees an apocalypse where humans are dying for an unknown reason.

Kala, being unsure about this event and as none of the angels created by The Mother can interfere with the natural flow of time and fate of the universe, Maaya, his sister, the angel of illusion, lies and deception, suggests him to bear a child with a human, so that the child will have the powers of an angel and will be beyond the laws of The Mother.

Little does Kala knows, he is not stopping it, he is starting the destruction.

CHAPTER ONE

CHAPTER EKAM

Legend says, before the universe that we know existed, Mother and Father were the only two celestial beings. Father was destroyed by Mother during a heated battle between the two celestials. Father's spine was separated and was stuck to the floor in the Throne room. Mother later created angels and were then assigned different responsibilities. It was never intended to create life on Earth, but a mistake made by one of the angels resulted in creating life on Earth.

9 years earlier:

The rain had just stopped pouring, streets are empty and wet. Street lights blink continuously leaving low lights on streets than usual.

Within the low light, Subash was running for his life with a bag wrapped around his body, holding it with his hands near to his chest, struggling to keep up the pace.

He stopped to grab some air, he bent holding his knees with his hands and struggling to catch some air.

He looked around, he found two dumpsters painted blue, filled with garbage, he also saw a kid trying to find something in one of the dumpsters.

The kid was a little 10-year-old girl wearing a white gown with dirt and filth all over. Hair till shoulder tangled, and face covered with dirt.

He looked back and found the goons approaching him.

He ran and hid behind the dumpster.

He saw the kid getting food out of the dumpster, sitting next to it. She blew air from her mouth while rubbing the food gently with her fingers.

He looked at her with pity filled in his eyes. “She might have not eaten from days.” He thought.

She saw him hiding behind the dumpster opposite her, he kept his pointing finger on his lips and whispered to her to be quiet.

She went back tearing the pieces of her bread and eating it.

Soon the goons approached the place. They stopped running, they looked around and couldn’t find the way that he went. The streets were empty and silent except for the sound of crickets.

One of the 3 goons looked at the girl and asked: “Hey you...”

The girl didn’t respond, she started eating the bread that she pulled out from the dumpster.

“Hey?? Are you deaf? You homeless girl... don’t you hear me shouting?” One of the goons shouted at her.

She lifted her head and looked at him.

“Did you see anyone coming this way?” He asked.

She turned her head off him and started eating again.

“You are dead meat!” The goon shouted angrily and walked towards the girl.

He grabbed her tangled hair and lifted her.

She was shouting in pain as Subhash was looking helplessly at her hiding behind the dumpster.

“I am asking you the last time! Did you or not see someone running this way?”.

She lifted her head and looked at the goon angrily.

The goon looked at her eyes, he left her hair, in shock.

He moved back... scratching his spine.

"What happened?" One of the other goons asked.

"Her eyes, they are glowing red" he replied stuttering nervously.

Subhash saw the rage in her eyes. Her eyes turned red and her pupils turned narrow. Her eyes looked like the eyes of a hungry predator. Subash was astonished and frightened at the same time.

Subhash couldn't bear the sight of grown men torturing a kid. Just before he surrendered, a knife slid through her hand sleeves, she stabbed the one who was holding her hair on his thigh.

He was shouting in pain. she pulled the knife out, continued stabbing and tearing the pieces of meat on the thigh repeatedly.

Blood was everywhere around them on the pavement. She held the blood-dripping knife in her hand, looked at the other two goons, and made a 'grrr' like sound, that sounded as similar as an angry cat.

Her teeth were sharp and pointy. They were standing in front of her in shock, while the third one was holding his leg and shouting in pain. She ran towards them, being scared of her red eyes and sharp teeth like a devil, they ran away.

She turned around and started walking back towards her food.

Subash came running to her.

"Wha...how...? who are you?" he asked in surprise.

She started walking back towards the dumpster.

She picked up the bun and started eating it again.

"Wait... don't eat that. Let me buy you some food" Subash said.

She picked a paper from the dumpster.

She cleaned the knife with the paper. She rolled up her sleeves and kept the knife back in its sheath.

She looked at Subash and said, "Let's go".

As gratitude, he took her to the nearby food court and bought her some fresh food and gave her some money.

she extended her arms and took the bag with food.

"Don't you want money?" Subash asked.

She didn't respond and started walking back.

Subash walked to her and held her with his arms, and sat on his knees, looking into her eyes.

"I wish I could do much more than this child, is there anything which I can do?" he asked.

She was looking at him desperately.

"Child, I will give you whatever you ask if it's in my reach, you saved my life, that's the least I can do," he said.

"Home" She replied.

"Usually, I would handover you to child services, but looks like that's not the correct place for you," Subash said and continued

"Probably it's for the best... home would make you grow as a person and I could teach you morals, the morals that I didn't get to teach to my daughter".

"Let's get moving before someone sees us," he said and they left the place.

He took her home to his home.

His home is a small two-bedroom, two-bath independent house.

She stepped into the home as Subash closed the door on her behind. She was looking around the home in wonder.

"You live alone?" She asked looking at him.

"Being a widower and no kids, yes, I live alone" he replied.

He smiled and spoke. "Now this is your home too".

"Here... wear these... I do not have anything that fits you... but this is my cousin's daughter's sweater... it might be a little loose... but this will do for now..." he said extending his hand with the sweater and knickers in his hand.

"You might want to freshen up, I have switched on the water heater. I will make your bed meanwhile" he said.

When he walked out of her bedroom she took shower, came out and was staring at the portrait of his wife on the wall.

"She was my wife, she was dead" he replied.

"Do you miss her?" She asked.

"Every day. Not a single day goes by without me thinking about her. She was the love of my life. She was brutally killed..." Subash said and stopped talking suddenly.

"Sorry, I was getting emotional. Let's put you in bed" he said and took her to her bedroom.

Her room was small, with cartoons painted on the walls with a crib and a bed on opposite sides of the room.

"Whose room is it?" she asked.

"I had it ready so that my son or daughter, but...." Subash paused and continued.

"But, it is your now." He said.

He put her on the bed, tucked her, and was walking out of her room.

"I forgot to ask, what's your name?" he asked.

"Avinashya" she replied.

"Well, Avinashya, I am Subhash, good night," he said and switched off the lights in her room.

He sat down in the living room having a drink and looking at his wife's photo. She was a beautiful woman.

The thoughts of his wife came running in his head. He recalled the incident of a person killing his wife as his tears rolled over his eyes.

A knife was held up against her throat and slither while Subhash was tied up and beaten, all he could do was watch her die helplessly.

She was trying to reach Subhash with her hand while she was dying.

He slept on the couch thinking about him missing his wife, the moments that they spent together.

It was 10 in the morning when he woke up and Avinashya woke him up. It's her daily routine that woke him up.

She was practising a kind of martial arts outside in the garden. Subash saw her throwing hands and legs in the air flipping and flying continuously. She looked a lot flexible to him.

Neighbours surrounded their house watching her play with knives.

"Hey Avinashya, good morning," Subhash said smiling at her.

She didn't stop, and she didn't even respond. She kept practising.

"What are you doing Avinashya?" He asked.

"Practising," she said.

"I can see that, what are you practising?" he said

"It's called Jaji" she replied.

"Well, that's great! it would be better if you come in" he said.

"No" she replied.

"What do you mean no?" He replied and walked to her.

He stopped her from playing with her knives on the streets.

He ran towards her and grabbed her with his arms.

“Hey, hey, I understand that it’s important to you to practice... if you want to practice something do it in the home, where there will be a lesser number of the audience...” he said.

“She is my cousin’s daughter,” he said looking at the neighbours taking her into the house.

He sat her down on the couch and asked, “So where did you learn this ‘Jaja’ skill”.

“It’s Jaji, my mother taught me this. She said that it was angel’s martial art.” She replied.

“Wow! So, where’s your mother now?”

“She left me.”

“I am sorry about that. Anyways, you have a dad now.”

He stood up and walked towards the kitchen.

He started cooking food for his office while she was sitting on the couch watching cartoons excitedly. Suddenly she shouted in pain holding her right hand.

“What happened? Are you okay?” he ran to her and asked.

She pointed at her hand and showed a cut that was bleeding badly.

“Whoa! That’s a really deep cut, let’s go to the hospital.”

Subash and Avinashya were rushed to the nearest hospital and underwent treatment and started from hospital to back home.

Subash walked towards his car which is at the entrance of the hospital and went back home.

CHAPTER TWO

19 years earlier, somewhere in another REALM:

Kala, the angel of time and fate, King of the angels and protector of the realms, foresees an event where the people on Earth die of an unknown cause. that's going to happen.

People were falling off like leaves in autumn.

The view not only gave him chills but he was also terrified to see it. He opened his eyes with terror.

He is a 14 feet mystic warrior, wearing a sleeveless shield that glows in white. A muscled-up body with beard on his face and a scar of sword on his left cheek. A crown on his head containing the king jewel called Marola, a stone made of the very first elements that were created in the universe, whose power emission is enough to brighten a whole planet.

"Disaster! I must stop it!" Kala thought and stood from his throne.

He vanished into thin air and disappeared into sprinkles.

He visited Mruthyu, the angel of destruction and death. Mruthyu was wearing a black robe with a hood over his head covering his skull face and a scythe in his left hand with 3 skulls and an hourglass hanging over his robe.

He was standing, looking at a grave with the scythe. That place was covered with dark raging clouds, echoing with the screams of the sinned souls. Graves all around the place till the eye can see.

Sensing the arrival of Kala, he started speaking.

"Time has come, isn't it brother?" The Mruthyu said in a deep voice.

"You knew? It is your doing, isn't it?" Kala asked.

"It's humans" Mruthyu turned and shouted in anger.

His hallow eyes were glowing red in the fire. Skies roaring with lighting as loud as his voice was, as he cooled down the glowing red fire over his eyes came down.

"It's humans and their doing, I must collect their souls and punish them for their sins after their death," Mruthyu said and continued.

"Anyways, why would I interfere in the matters of those puny insects! I am much more superior than that. Or did you forget that?" Mruthyu shouted in his demonic voice in rage.

Skies were roaring with thunders and his skull face started glowing in deep red flame showing his rage.

Kala took a step back in fright.

"I am sorry brother, please forgive me. Please cool down" Kala bowed and continued

"Is there any way to stop it?" Kala asked raising his head back.

Mruthyu laughed and said "Even the mightiest of angels cannot stop it. It's nature, Kala. Did you stop the extinction of huge lizards which are now called dinosaurs? It's the natural flow of time. We should not intervene. Remember? That's The Mother's very first law. We are all bound by the laws of her."

"I recommend you don't get tempted like you always do and help them. We are keepers of laws of the Universe to maintain balance." Mruthyu said.

Kala turned and started walking back in disappointment and he vanished in sprinkles.

CHAPTER THREE

CHAPTER TREENI

6 months earlier, SSB HEADQUARTERS:

"Do you know why we called you here miss? Avinashya?" SSB chief Mukesh Tripathi asked and continued.

"Avinashya, we know that you applied for other services in central government. But I had your resume pulled into SSB."

"Let me be honest with you..."

"Avinashya, we know who you are and what you are. We saw you in a surveillance camera taking out 4 armed robbers in a bank with your bare hands. God was you fast!!"

"We did our homework, we enquired about you. Don't worry your secret is safe with us" he continued.

"On behalf of SSB, we request you to consider joining our organization."

"Before you make a decision, you need to know a little bit about us too. We are the Society of Supernatural Investigations. I am the founder of this organization."

"Supernatural? What do you mean sir?" Avi asked.

"It means what it means... we investigate supernatural beings and their powers." He replied.

"You must be kidding... are there any such things?" she asked.

"We are a team backed by governments of multiple nations to investigate dangerous cults and their activities that may be dangerous to the society."

"I can enclose more details about this operation but I need your decision before I do as this is confidential information." He said.

She was confused, she couldn't decide what she should choose.

"I need some time to think sir," she said.

"Take all the time you need Avinashya, but never discuss this with anyone, not your father, not your boyfriend Mahesh. As I said, we know everything about you. So, believe me, we will know if you do." He said.

He gave her the pen drive containing surveillance footage of her.

She went to her flat where she lives alone. She plugged in the pen drive on her laptop and played the video.

She never felt the energy field around her when she was aroused with anger.

For the first time, she saw herself. In the footage where she was standing at the counter and 4 robbers entered the bank shooting in the air.

As they enter a guard tried stopping them. They shot down the guard on their way in. They held a little girl at gunpoint and asked everyone to drop their mobile phones in the bag.

The little girl bit the hand of the one holding her and ran towards her mom. He shook his hand off in pain. He got mad and shot her.

Avinashya standing there and watching all this triggered her anger. A great circle of energy field visible enough started appearing around her.

Nature sensing the presence of supernatural power on the face of the earth started responding with air whooshing around her.

She took a knife from her handbag, ran and cut the throat of the robber who shot the girl.

“Down” she shouted.

Her voice was distorted as a demon would speak.

Everyone in the bank kneeling till then laid on the ground in fear.

Bullets were not able to pierce her energy field. As soon as the bullet hit her energy field they started melting and falling in the liquid metal form.

Once the robbers’ guns magazines went empty, she lifted the dead robber, she threw him towards the other robbers. They have fallen.

She slid over to them on her knees. Her knife turned blazing hot red. She pierced a robber’s neck with one hand, pulled another knife from her bag and stabbed it on his forehead. He fell and was dead on spot with melted steel on his forehead dripping over his eyes.

She stood up to a view of people getting up and afraid of her. Dropped the knife in her hand, which turned shape out because of its melting and turned black as it cooled down.

Everyone was staring at her like she was some demon they are witnessing for the first time.

As she walked towards the counter to take her bag, people started giving her way in fear.

“Tough crowd,” she said and she left the bank.

Avinashya found something more than an energy in that video. She rewound a few seconds and paused the video.

She was shocked to see herself when she paused. When she did, she saw herself with a sharp corner tooth coming out of her lips, eyes glowing in red as fire, face and body turned as black as night.

No wonder the people who saw were scared to death.

19 years earlier, somewhere in another realm:

Kala was pacing in the throne room, thinking how he could prevent the great war. He started thinking himself.

While he was thinking, Maaya, the angel of deception and lies entered by presenting herself in the form of sprinkles with a pale white complexion and pretty white gown, hair till her knees, and 13ft in height.

She is a beautiful angel with eyes glowing with the spark that ties any mighty in her bounds and the smile that mesmerize the toughest of the gods. She has a white parrot resting on her shoulder. Her mere entry brings the fragrance that sets one's mind into sleep.

"Seems like someone's having a rough day," said Maaya in her soothing and calm voice.

"Not a good time sister" Kala replied.

"Brother, what siblings are for if we don't share the troubles."

"It doesn't concern you sister. You might as well leave".

Maaya floated towards Kala leaving a white sprinkling smoke behind her as she floated.

She touched Kala with her hand and stopped him from pacing.

Kala cooled down as she touched him.

"There's something that's bothering me, but it should stay between us," he said.

"You have my word brother," said Maaya in her calm voice.

"I've foreseen a future. Great destruction on Earth" he said

"Earth? You mean Humans?" She laughed and continued.

"Those useless creatures! They wouldn't change would they!" she said and continued.

"It happened twice earlier, why bother now brother?" She asked.

"Saarga created them for some reason Mother knows why. But at end of the day, they are living beings who would need help from us. The Angels." Kala said and continued.

"I saw it, sister. It's happening and I am unable to find a way to stop it from happening without my intervention" Kala replied.

Maya stood still and started thinking.

"Being bound to Mother's laws we shouldn't intervene with the flow of time. If we cannot involve and stop this destruction, who can?" Kala asked.

"So, you want someone with our powers who can stop this destruction but doesn't break any of The Mother's laws right?" Maaya asked and continued.

"The only option I see here is you having a child with one of the humans, that way the child will not be bound to Mother's laws but will have angel's powers."

"And who could be the best option for having a child other than the mighty king of angels," Maaya said.

"How could that not be an intervention with the flow of time?" Kala asked.

"You were only giving birth to a person who can save the earth, protect the earth. Not only this one time, throughout the existence. So, this one intervention could save Earth a million times. Think about it." Maaya said.

CHAPTER FOUR

CHAPTER CHATVAARI

19 years earlier, somewhere in another realm:

"Brother, all these laws wouldn't matter if there's nothing left which you are supposed to protect," Maaya said in her soothing voice and continued.

"Mother created this universe, she's now in sleep since many millenniums. A day will come, when she'll wake up and notice that we didn't try to stop the destruction from happening, she's going to be much more disappointed than breaking a small law."

"If it has at least 1% chance preventing it, then I suggest that you do it," she said rubbing his shoulders.

"I think I got the idea, thank you, sister," Kala said and walked away from that place with confidence and a smile on his face.

Current day, somewhere in the woods, dungeon of the red priest:

"She has grown into a powerful woman. Now it's about time to initiate our plan and kill her and cause the destruction." Red Priest said in his distorted voice.

He was in a robe with a hoodie and a mask covering his face. Red paint all over his face.

He was facing a wall where all the candles are present. The picture of a person with horns on his head sitting on a throne with a demonic face on the wall.

"Hail The Father" the red cult chanted in unison.

"We are just humans; she is an angel in the form of a human. How can we stop her?" one of the members of the cult asked.

"We may not be able to stop her, but we have another option though." The Red Priest said showing Vulcan the Russian virologist.

He is a 5.7' fair looking and average built guy with messed up hair.

"We have a weapon, a virus. We use that to kill her and everyone else. The great plan of Kala would fail then. Earth along with his favourite daughter, everyone would die. Along with that, we have the help from angels to cause this destruction." The Red Priest said laughing.

19 years earlier, somewhere in India:

"I'm leaving, Indhu," Subhash said while packing his bag to get going to his office.

"Subhash, you forgot your lunch," said Indhu running out from the kitchen with a lunch box in her hand.

She was in her night robe, with a hair bun. She was a beautiful woman with a fair complexion with a beautiful smile that never leaves her face and was also 7 months pregnant.

"Thanks, mwah" he kissed her and left home.

Subhash was waiting outside a house which is of a politician Marthand Raj and the house was painted white with 4 security guards outside a huge door.

A car came out of the house and Subhash started following it from a safe distance.

He saw the car going into a guest house. He parked the car somewhere near the guest house and walked towards it.

He took his camera from his bag and jumped over a wall. He landed on a path that takes to the garden of the guest house.

He went near a window to have a better look, he saw 3 men walking into a bedroom, and Army chief Devansh Patnaik is one among them.

He got surprised to see an Army Chief with a politician.

Once they went into the room, Subhash jumped over the window and followed them towards the bedroom unnoticed.

He hid behind the bedroom entrance and was trying to see what was happening inside.

He saw Vulcan tied up in a chair and beaten to death. He started taking pictures of them.

"Did he tell?" Devansh the army chief asked a goon who was guarding the guy in the chair.

"No sir, I even tried 3rd degree, he doesn't say a word." The goon replied.

"I got to know. He had the formula stored somewhere. If we can get that, he is of no use to us" Marthand said.

Marthand picked up an iron rod and hit Vulcan with it.

"Where's the formula," Marthand asked.

Vulcan spitted the blood in his mouth and looked intensively towards Marthand.

"Go ahead and kill me, you will never get your hands on my formula," Vulcan said in a Russian accent.

"Oh, trust me, you will" Marthand said.

He took out his mobile and called someone.

"Kill his daughter," Marthand said to the guy on the phone.

"Don't you dare touch my daughter!" Vulcan said by forcing himself to get up from the chair.

"Vulcan, look at your daughter, remind her one last time before she's dead. You have two options in front of you. You either give up the formula and live, or you'll die, your daughter dies and your wife dies" Marthand said showing Vulcan his phone.

"Please don't kill her, promise me," Vulcan asked crying.

"You have my word," Devansh said.

"Locker # 202, Bank of Business, 3rd Avenue, Moscow. The passcode is 191812221114" Vulcan said.

"Confirm me if you find it," Marthand said to the guy who's been online on the phone and disconnected the call.

After a few minutes, Marthand's mobile rang and he lifted the call and put it on speaker.

"There's a book here," he said.

"Kill him," said Marthand to the goon.

Devansh and Marthand walked out of the bedroom, Subhash hid behind the couch.

The goon who was guarding him took his gun out and pointed it on Vulcan's head. Before he shot him, Subhash walked in and hit him with his steel lunch box on his head.

The goon turned back and pointed his gun towards Subhash. Subhash then knee kicked him in his nuts, picked the iron rod and hit him on his head.

The goon has fallen and lost his consciousness. Subhash then untied him and took him to his home.

Subhash closed all the doors and windows in his home, his wife Indhu helped Vulcan in first aid and dressing his wounds.

Subhash switched on his voice recorder.

"Tell me everything, start with your name," Subhash said placing the recorder on the table pointing towards Vulcan.

Vulcan started speaking.

"My name is Vulcan Smirnov. I am a Russian virologist. I used to work for 2day Pharma for 10 years. My research is to develop a virus that can be used against any pathogen viruses which cause diseases."

"If my research is successful, one virus can kill any disease like AIDS caused by a virus or any other microorganisms."

"For this to work, I designed a virus which can mutate as per the conditions of the pathogen virus. During the process, I accidentally created a virus which can mutate but is harmful to the host body instead".

"This means, if this virus is injected, instead of killing the disease-causing organism, it will kill the human."

"During my tests, I tested the virus on a lab rat, it was normal for 1 hour, but after that, the organs started failing. And the rat died in 2hours after it's been introduced to the host body."

"Andrei, my colleague, saw it and sold the information to a North Korean spy."

"They've been hunting me down since then, I've changed my identity and have gone underground. I don't know how they found me but Marthand and Devansh tied up with the spy and tried to get their hands on this virus."

"Just before you saved me, they were threatening me to kill my daughter. I have given him a wrong locker which on unlocking triggers an alarm to the bank security for unauthorized access."

"The locker contains nothing but a thesis draft that I submitted during my PhD. I did it to save my daughter."

"I don't know if there are many like him over there, I just want to save my daughter."

"I cannot have them get the virus either. It will endanger the world if it went into the wrong hands. Please help me to help you"

CHAPTER FIVE

CHAPTER PANCHA

19 years earlier, Somewhere in India:

"Vulcan, let's get you somewhere safer," Subhash said after his confession.

"Thanks for saving me," Vulcan said.

"Subhash, you are supposed to take me for my checkup remember?" Indhu asked.

"Yes, I remember, you can join us," Subhash said.

"Vulcan do you mind if we take a detour to the hospital for Indhu's checkup," he asked Vulcan.

"No problem," Vulcan replied.

Three of them left in a car to the hospital.

"We are here for our regular checkup with Dr. Sushree," Subhash said to the receptionist.

"I'm sorry, Dr. Sushree has passed away in a car accident yesterday. We have Dr. Sathish, her temporary replacement. I can arrange a meeting with him if you like!" Receptionist asked.

"I'm sorry to hear it, we are good to meet Dr. Sathish. Thank you" said Subhash.

Indhu and Subhash were sent to Dr. Sathish while Vulcan was waiting in the common waiting area.

"Hello Dr. Sathish, we are here for our regular checkup," Subhash said.

It was none other than the angel of time and fate himself in an apron and his human form.

Dior was standing next to him in his nurse uniform checking the sonogram machine for the checkup.

"Doctor, the baby is showing no sign of heartbeat," the Nurse said and handed over the reports to Sathish while Subhash and Indhu were waiting outside the room.

"Send them in Nurse," Sathish asked.

"Mr. & Mrs. Subhash, I'm afraid I have bad news," Sathish said in a sad tone.

Subhash and Indhu started holding hands.

"What is it, doctor? Is the baby fine?" Indhu asked.

"Well, it's about that, the baby is showing no signs of heartbeat, in other words, the baby isn't alive." He said in a sad tone.

"No, it can't be, how can it happen. Can you please check one more time?" Subash started asking in a sad tone.

"I am 100% certain Mr. Subash" Sathish replied.

Indhu started crying after hearing the news. Subhash put his hand around his wife and started soothing her.

"It's ok Indhu," he said.

"We have to remove the baby's body. Else it will be a problem for the mother" Sathish said.

"Mrs. Indhu, I would like to talk to you alone before you accept this procedure." He said.

19 years earlier, somewhere in another realm:

The Mruthyu was sitting on a throne that appears to be a grave. The throne is black and with blazing fire on the backrest. He stood up from the throne holding his scythe in his right hand.

“Do you know what this hourglass is for Maaya?” The Mruthyu asked in his demonic voice while walking down the steps towards her as she appeared in sprinkles in front of his throne sensing her arrival.

“It says that you decide who’s time is up, isn’t it? She replied.

“No, Maaya. I was killed by our very own mother. I was the firstborn Before you, before Kala.” He said and continued.

“Look at you, all sparkly and beautiful, look at Kala, all misty and muscled up. Now, look at me.” He said.

His robe started burning leaving holes exposing his body.

I am a skeleton in a red-hot fire, I am ugly. My name is Mruthyu, which means death.

This hourglass, mother presented it to me to tell that the time cannot be turned back, even if you’re the almighty. Time is superior. You’ve to accept it and move on.

I have not asked for this life, yet here I am doing something which I don’t want to. Whereas my younger brother is sitting on the throne as a king of angels.

Despite all these, I am not furious, you know why? Because we belong to one family. I saw you advising Kala about the destruction. I hope you are not misleading Kala.

“Brother, why would I do that, I am one of the family members. I too want to stop the destruction. I will never do such thing ever.” Maaya replied.

“Good to hear that, that’s the only reason I summoned you. You can now leave.” Mruthyu said.

Maya vanished into white sprinkles and left Celestial Pit.

Present, somewhere in the forest:

"Vulcan, my friend" The red priest invited him towards the statue of The Father where he was standing.

The red priest continued.

You know how we talked about creating a world that will be a better place with all the diseases cured! Now it's time. Humans are the disease to this beautiful planet of ours.

Create the virus. Let's make the earth a better place. But the question is...

How do we make the earth a better place if everyone dies? The red priest asked.

"Well, it's possible. The virus takes a year to kill the organs, break down cells, and finally kill a human. But the virus when introduced into a pregnant lady, the baby will adapt to the virus in the womb itself hence the baby will remain unaffected by the virus." Vulcan explained.

"A new generation, in a year we will have a handful of babies, using them we will create a new generation, teach them morals, start the civilization from the scratch, creating an alter creation against the nature. Evolution of mankind from the beginning again." The red priest said and started laughing loudly.

CHAPTER SIX

CHAPTER SHAT

A few millenniums earlier, somewhere in another realm:

"What are you working on Saarga?" Maaya asked while appearing out of thin air in sparkles in the "Room of Mirrors".

Saarga ignored her visit and continued working. He was holding a wand that controls the mirrors in the room. He was facing a mirror and waving his hand while creating a blueprint for something that he was working on.

He was thin and short with long hair and a pearl band around his head. He was wearing a scarf around his neck that falls in front. A wand in his hand which was made of the branch from the tree of Wisdom.

Maaya on appearing said, "You have a nice view here... Room of Mirrors, which is filled with mirrors all over the room. You get to visit all the realms as you wish through these mirrors.

You also have a white ocean with a small island in it.

You also get to have fruits from the "Wisdom Tree" when it blossoms for the first time in every millennium. You get to try the food that we angels eat before they grow completely.

You must be having fun Saarga.." Maaya said.

"Maaya, what are you doing here?" Saarga asked by looking at her.

"I like the view Saarga, and I also wanted to meet you and see how you are doing." She continued.

The pleasant sound of waves, aah! What I wouldn't give to be here my whole life. Not everyone is as lucky as you are.

She walked towards the blueprint that Saarga was working on. She looked at the blueprint standing beside him by resting her left hand on his right shoulder and continued speaking.

"This looks confusing.. what is it Saarga?" She asked with curiosity.

"It's a gift for The Mother, since she stopped using her powers, I thought I could make something for her which helps her in transportation from one realm to the other." He said.

"That's clever, she is getting old and using her powers is only reducing her life by creating a void. It's something she can use." She continued.

"So, what is it exactly?" She asked.

"I named it "The Veiled Bird". It's a transport machinery that takes mother to any of the realms that she wanted to visit without anyone noticing her arrival." He said.

"Nice." She said as sparks from her left hand started appearing on the top of her fingers.

"Saarga, look at me." She said.

Saarga turned back and was looking at Maaya as her eyes turned blue.

"Why haven't you gifted me anything like this?" She asked.

He waved his hand and made a mirror come by and stop in front of him. He extended his hand into the mirror and took out a cage with a parrot in it.

"Well, I created this bird. I call this bird a white parrot. It serves you as a messenger, it can also vanish and appear out of thin air.. just like you." He said showing a parrot.

Maaya took the cage and released the parrot by opening the cage. The parrot flew and sat on her shoulder as she started rubbing her neck.

"I love this bird Saarga. But I have one more thing that I have to ask." She said.

"Tell me, it's my job to create and maintain things for the angels. Just tell me what you want and I will get it done"

"I want life. Angelic figures without any powers created on realm # 7". She said.

Saarga looked at her shocked and moved back by taking her hand off his shoulder.

"Maaya, I only design objects for celestial beings and the thing you asked is not one of them. I am sorry I cannot do that" he said.

"Saarga, you know why mother made you thin and short unlike the rest of the angels. While she gave others the brute force, she gave you wisdom, she gave to the power to create things." She continued.

She doesn't want you to explore your powers and that's why she restricted you for making only celestial objects for us.

"Why do you even want to create these creatures? Realm #7 is filled with giant Lizards. These creatures won't make a day without any powers in front of those lizards." He said

Besides, lizards are our least problem. I wouldn't do anything that's against the mother's law. It will surely make her angry.

She held his face in her hands and gently stroked his hair with her hands.

"What are you doing?" He asked confused.

"If you create these creatures, you will be the king of these creatures, then I can be the queen for them." She kissed him on his lips.

He pulled himself from the kiss and walked back.

"You are my sister, what are you doing?" He asked shocked.

"Sister? There's no relationship like mother, brother or sister Saarga... it's just part of mother's plan to restrict us... restrict us from having kids, having sons or daughters." She continued.

"She is the almighty, but she couldn't give any of us complete powers as she thought we could take her over."

"All these restrictions are to keep her position as an almighty intact. She never wanted you to create any other things but celestial objects."

"Does any of these make sense to you Saarga? it's our chance to put an end to Mother's restrictions. Let's conceive a child together. Let's start a new religion where you, me and our unborn child will be the immortal king for these mortals."

"It's not true, she limited our powers because she knew that we weren't capable of handling the burden of having all of it and also.." he was interrupted by Maaya.

"Do you even make sense to yourself? Saarga, we both were brought to life in one single instant. I know what you are and you don't deserve this. Trust me in this.." she said and touched him on his shoulders with her left arm.

Sprinkles out of her fingers appeared, the eyes of Saarga were dilated and was looking into the eyes of Maaya.

"I know you want it too, don't restrict it.. the restrictions you are having from The Mother are enough already.." she said and kissed him again on his lips.

Thunders started raging as they started feeling each other. Clouds were roaring in the dark skies of Paradise.

Things escalated quickly as they started having sex. None of the angels knows the reason behind the sudden outburst of the weather.

Maaya and Saarga were laying under a sheet on a bed. Saarga stood up and walked to a canvas that was at the corner of the room.

Maaya stood up from the bed, holding the sheets against her naked body.

Maaya waved her hand which re-dressed her in her pretty white gown. She walked towards Saarga and stood behind him.

"What are you working on, the bird thing?" She asked.

"No, I named them Humans," he said.

CHAPTER SEVEN

CHAPTER SAPTA

A few millenniums earlier, somewhere in another realm:

Maaya and Saarga were lying on a bed made of clouds in the Celestial Paradise covering themselves in a single sheet.

"It's been three years, how close are we to creating humans?" Maaya asked still lying on the bed.

"It's not that easy.. we've to clone an angel, remove their powers to the last cell and then only we can send them to multiply on Earth." Saarga replied and continued.

"What was your solution for mother and the great Lizards though?" He asked.

"Lizards are our least concern, but add this to your creation" Maaya replied with an evil smile on her face extending her hand.

"What is it?" Saarga asked.

"It is the ash fallen from the Mighty Flaming sword. Add this to your creation" Maaya said.

"Why?" Saarga asked in confusion.

"Legend says, that there was The Father before we were created. Mother had to destroy him as he was feeding on the souls of living beings. And the flaming sword that we see is the spine of our Father." She said.

"Who told you this?" Saarga asked.

"I did my research," Maaya said with an evil smile on her face.

19 years earlier, the ostracised caves, somewhere in another realm:

Ostracized caves are located on the bank of the river called "Muzak" which is a divine ale for the angels.

The caves are giant with Ealcans a celestial bird evolved from Vulcans and eagles hovering around them screeching for the bones surrounding the caves in the deep dark clouds raging with thunders.

The outside of the caves is filled with decomposed bones of the angels, the bones were decomposed with tiny holes in them where bones eating organisms were crawling on them.

The shore of the Muzak consists of sand which has tiny sand granules and fallen asteroids like rocks structures.

Curse on the ostracized caves makes shore unbearable to angels. The foul smell that emits from the decomposed bones would melt the organs in the angels.

She was standing in front of a huge rock on a pit supported by the two rock pillars on either side of the pit.

A huge beast like structure resting on the rock snoring in her sleep facing the opposite side of the entrance to the cave.

As Maaya presented herself, she smelled power, she rubbed her nose with her hands and opened her eyes.

The eyes of the beast were wide opened with a narrow retina and a brown eyeball around it.

"I smell an angel" she shouted excitedly in a deep voice resulting in the echoes in the caves.

"I think you smell yourself, sister, you're an angel too.. did you forget?" Maaya replied.

She turned back and sat on the rock. She was a huge beast like an angel with 32ft in height, clothes made of bones tied together with leaves straws on the island. Hair turned brown, tangled and long enough to use it as a rope to tie someone with it.

She saw Maaya in front of her standing, she extended her hand to grab her. Her hand was big enough to hold a 14ft angel in its wrist with nails filled with sand from the shore of Muzak.

As she tried catching her, Maaya vanished and presented herself behind Gaia.

"Sister, none of the angels can vanish and appear as they please.. so, it might be easy for you to get hold of them but..." she was interrupted by the incoming hand of Gaia which hit the rocks of the cave leaving a claw-shaped hole on the rocks as she vanished again.

"We can do this all day.. or we can.." a foot bigger than her hand stomped on her.

Maaya stopped the foot on midair from stomping her using her hands and creating an energy field around her.

Maaya was struggling to control the brute force of her foot trying to stomp her.

She tried speaking.

"I am here to talk sister, think... why would any angel visit this place even after knowing what you are capable of... I got you a deal, I can make you an angel like us" she said struggling.

"Lies, I know who you are, you and your fake promises" She shouted and tried much harder to break the energy field that Maaya created.

"I am telling the truth sister, believe me... what shall I do to make you believe me?" She asked still struggling to control the field and stopping her feet.

Gaia removed her feet slowly from the energy field and placed them on the floor of the cave filled with gravel stones.

"Thanks, the weight almost started to crush me," Maaya said sighing in relief.

"Tell me your darkest secret, to believe you," Gaia asked.

"How would you know if I am telling the truth?" Maaya asked.

"I wouldn't, but that's the risk you have to take," Gaia said laughing.

"I want to be the almighty" She replied and continued.

"I have created humans with the ashes from the mighty flaming sword many millenniums ago to wake up The Father. But he never did. Does "The Father" exist only in the legend or is it true. I cannot wait any longer. I want you to show me the path of waking The Father up."

"So that he would destroy The Mother. I knew he is capable of doing that. If he succeeds, I would be his favourite daughter as I woke him up. And he would let me rule some of The Mother's creation."

"I know that you have the answer for my desire," Maaya said.

"You might have succeeded in establishing your father's powers in humans, but the powers are nothing if they are not triggered by divinity," Gaia said.

"What should I do then?" Maaya asked.

"Do what you are best at. Create an illusion in Kala's head. Show him destruction, an apocalypse. Make him think, he must save The Mother's creation. Have him conceive a child with a human. That shall do it. That child will awaken The Father." Gaia said.

"Why Kala?" Maaya asked.

"He is the mightiest among the angels, only he wields the power to wake up the father who was resting in the souls of humans," Gaia replied.

Maaya vanished from the caves with a smile on her face.

"I always hated you angels and your dirty laws. The path that I showed you, not only wakes up The Father. It's also destruction for all the angels including The Mother." Gaia thought herself laughing menacingly.

CHAPTER EIGHT

CHAPTER ASHTA

19 years earlier, somewhere in India:

"What is it Prayogya?" Prof. Kundan asked.

Behind him, Prayogya was standing in his glowing shield with the crown on his head and a huge scabbard on his back holding the mightiest of the swords.

The sword is 8ft in length "The Soul Taker" glowing blazing red. An axe made of the dead angels' skulls, black with a diamond handlebar in his right hand.

"I am sorry for my sudden visit your highness; I had a message for you from Kala," Prayogya replied.

"First things first, turn into human form" Kundan commanded.

As he did, Prayogya turned into a human form leaving his face and crown intact.

"I cannot talk to you unless you turn yourself completely, it's a high risk to divinity if anyone sees you like this.." Kundan said.

Prayogya turned himself into a complete human by turning his shield into a black jacket, crown into a bean cap, sword into a cane and axe into the handle for the cane.

"See I have another meeting that I should attend, let's talk on my way... if anyone asks, your name is Mahesh, you are a journalist taking my interview. Got it?" Kundan said.

"Understood your highness" he replied.

"Stop calling me that, call me professor," Kundan said.

They walked out from the room towards the car.

Kundan sat in the driver's cabin and started driving.

"So, tell me.. what is it?" Kundan asked.

"Professor, Kala wants to visit this realm for a divine deed. He is seeking your approval and suggestions in this regard." He said.

"For what purpose?" Kundan asked.

Prayogya in the form of Mahesh extended his left hand making the scroll appear out of nowhere.

He opened the scroll and started reading.

"Tatva, the angel of Realm Reacher's, and the bridge between Paradise and the realms, I, Kala writing this message to request permission in visiting realm #7. I have foreseen an apocalypse where the greater bad is going to happen in this realm and I request your permission to visit and stop it once and for all...

I do not intend to break any more laws than I am breaking already to stop this from happening. So, I cannot enter the realm without your permission and without notifying you.

Please send your approval with Prayogya."

He finished reading the scroll.

"How much sure he is about this so-called apocalypse happening?" Tatva in the form of Kundan asked.

"Enough to break the very first law of divinity" Prayogya replied.

Kundan stopped the car in shock.

He looked at Prayogya, as Prayogya released the scroll, it vanished into sprinkles.

"I am not asking as a messenger, I am requesting you as a brother, to both you and Kala, you must permit for this...".

Prayogya said.

"Ohh is it? Very good!! I thought giving permission isn't enough to get burnt into ashes by mother, now as you are including me in this... I foresee my future" Kundan said sarcastically.

"Brother, brother cool down... let me ask you one question... what good have we done since these creatures came into existence?" Prayogya continued.

A demon would rise from the graveyard pit on this earth, one of us come in a human form, kill it and go back... we are the reason that these many religions exist on this planet... do you know that? People are killing themselves to prove which religion is superior as they didn't know there is no such thing as "religion".

Now we have a chance, an opportunity to help these creatures not because it may expose us... because we are breaking it... with or without your help, this is happening.. will you help us save this planet?"

"Well, why read a scroll if you have a speech prepared!! Let's go home and talk..." Tatva in the form of Kundan said.

Same time, same location, house of Kundan:

Kundan arrived at his home, as he walked towards the giant door, it opened.

"Don't you think humans will notice if you're using powers to unlock the door?" Prayogya asked.

"Don't be silly... it's sensors. I unlocked it from my mobile phone." He replied.

Prayogya walked into the view of a big mansion filled with souvenirs from different timelines.

Paintings with kings that ruled the country during ancient times on top of his entertainment unit.

"Your highness..." Prayogya was interrupted by Tatva.

"Yes, these are my souvenirs from different times, and no, no human eye can see these" he replied.

He turned into his divine form with a long hair till his shoulders and a goatee beard. Wearing a long white gown with a red scarf around his neck, a book in his right hand that says "Secrets of Existence", a divine glow on his face emits the brightness that lights up the room.

"I lived here for centuries preaching what's good and what's bad, it had some effects on these creatures, can't we do that?" Tatva asked.

"Ohh really? By creating more religions?" Prayogya replied sarcastically.

"Brother, I have analyzed everything to see if we can prevent it from happening without breaking any laws, but these creatures evolved so much that they will always have proof left somewhere saying that an incident like this happened," Prayogya said.

"What if we kill the person who starts this, wipe off everyone's memory who's involved and pretend that it never happened?" Tatva asked.

"Kill a human? Brother, we are not supposed to kill any creature not celestial, not humans or any other creature on any of the realms. That's where a human, a mortal who's not bound to the laws of the mother comes in place." Prayogya explained.

"Alright! I authorize this... but I need more details.. how are we going to do it?" Tatva asked.

"For that, we need to find someone called Vulcan," Prayogya said.

"What's his full name?" Tatva asked opening the book of existence.

"Vulcan Smirnov".

As Tatva opened the book of existence, a gold colour light started emitting out of it with sparkles flowing upwards lighting up the whole room.

"I can't see anything," Prayogya said.

"Not only you, no one can see what the book says other than me, that's how Sarga created it," said Tatva and continued.

"You might want to close your eyes; the light can make you blind. It searches all the realms for the person or the creature you seek. That's why I have only guardsmen as visitors all these years".

He placed the book on the coffee table, placed his right hand on the book and uttered a mantra in his mouth by moving his left hand around the book.

A page turned open leaving the instructions on the book.

"Same instructions again, can't be used for personal gain etc. etc., I know, show me Vulcan already," Tatva said sarcastically.

A few pages turned open and stopped at a page revealing his identity.

"Vulcan Smirnov, he is a Russian virologist, born October 21st in Kyanda in Russia, has one daughter, and now hiding at a hotel here in Mumbai, an expert in genetics and a microbiologist," Tatva said and continued.

"This is his third life, first and second was in 1630 and 1820 respectively."

"His death.." He was interrupted by Prayogya.

"Isn't it one of the instructions? if not it should be! We shouldn't know a person's life span". Prayogya said.

"You shouldn't, but I can.." Tatva replied.

"Why do we need him?" He asked.

"According to Kala, he is the one who makes the virus that starts this apocalypse.

"Oh, so what's our plan?" Tatva asked.

"We've to abduct him," said Prayogya.

"And how do you suggest we do that?" Tatva asked.

"Do you have any human contacts who might help us in getting him?" Prayogya asked.

"I think I know one, I helped him during his worst phase to get over it. He said he is grateful for my help and he owes me one."

"Who is it?"

"He's a hitman by profession and his name is Ayukta".

A few moments later, location unknown, near the hotel where Vulcan's residing:

It was a night with stars in the sky visible. A narrow-wet road with traces of amounts of water from the rain, with street lights on either side on the pavement, and cars parked on the parking lane of the street.

Ayukta was sitting in his car parked opposite the hotel that Vulcan's been staying hiding himself among a few other cars that were already parked there.

Ayukta was a well-built 6.2ft person with a fair complexion and a skull tattoo on his left muscle which was visible because of the half sleeves t-shirt that he wore.

He picked up a cigarette and lightened it up, took a puff.

He picked his mobile from the socket and dialled a number.

"Hello Mr. Kundan, Ayukta here".

"I know, continue"

"The guy you asked me to abduct is not some common man.. are you aware of that?" Ayukta said to Kundan on phone.

"I know it Ayukta, tell me if it's not possible for you."

"I'm not talking about possibilities here, I did some digging and found out this guy is under the surveillance of North Koreans, the FBI, Interpol and our SSB... is he some terrorist?"

"How do you know that?"

"There are cars parked here, people taking shifts and monitoring his moments using hi-tech. An officer who was my friend while I was serving my time in jail told me that they might be monitoring a possible terrorist."

"How sure you are of him living here?" Ayukta asked.

"Why? Why do you ask that?"

"Because these people who are here just had a hunch and tracked he might be here, but you seemed pretty sure when you told me his location."

"So, what are you saying?"

"Well, here it is... it's impossible even to enter into the premises of this hotel without being noticed by the officers."

"Are you saying that we need high-security clearance?"

"If you put it that way... yes, it may help"

"Then help is on your way.."

"Thank you, Mr. Kundan," said Ayukta and disconnected the call.

Same time, same location, Kundan's house:

Kundan placed his mobile on the coffee table after talking with Ayukta.

"What is it Tatva?" Prayogya asked.

"Let's find a couple more who have great security clearance but not high to be on the radar."

"Why? is there a problem?"

"Yes, if our guy being monitored 24/7 and wanted by all the police organizations in the world a problem, then we have a big problem"

Tatva opened his book and placed it on the coffee table.

He closed his eyes and started circling his hand around the book.

It started glowing showing two persons on either of the pages.

"Marthand Raj, a politician, central home minister, Devansh Patnaik, chief of the army... I think these people would do" Tatva said looking at Prayogya.

Tatva transformed himself into the politician Marthand Raj who was in his mid-50s. And Prayogya turned himself into Devansh Patnaik, a well-built army chief.

"So, what's the plan here? Are they supposed to let us in just like that?" Prayogya asked.

"No, we are going to give a tip about Vulcan's whereabouts and mislead the officers and then abduct him"

"If that's the plan why did we even transform?"

"Even if we misled them, there might be a little surveillance and we shouldn't give them the opportunity of exposing ourselves and Vulcan may trust us seeing our profiles as a central minister and army chief," Tatva said.

"Let's summon Kala, we are starting this operation," he said.

As he finished saying that, Tatva held his hand near his heart and chanted in his mind a mantra that opened a portal in front of him.

A dark blue portal opened that directly connects to the throne room in the paradise where Kala was waiting for the invitation of Tatva.

Tatva and Prayogya walked into the portal. Kala sitting on the throne holding his head with his hand saw them walking into the throne room through a portal.

"Welcome back my friend, it's been a long time," Kala said.

"There's no time for pleasantries Kala, let's go," Tatva said.

The three of them walked back to earth through the portal. As Kala stepped on the face of the earth nature senses his presence by inviting him with a vigorous rain, ragging with thunders in the dark skies.

"Your highness," said Tatva and kneeled in front of him.

"We do not do it anymore Tatva, you may rise," Kala said and continued.

"As you know, I am here without mother's approval, so we have to be quick. We need the virus from Vulcan." Kala said.

"Why? I thought we just have to abduct him and have him killed. Why do we need his virus?" Tatva asked.

"I knew that he's on the radar of this realm's law caretakers. Some way or the other, even after we kill him, there's a chance that someone may find a way to recreate the virus. Then we would be back to page 1" Kala said.

"Then why wait? Let's get this guy" Prayogya said.

Tatva picked up his mobile from the coffee table and dialled the police helpline number 100.

One of the officers picked up.

"Hello officer, I knew about you keeping your radar on Vulcan the Russian virologist. I know his location." Tatva said.

"May I know your name, sir?" The officer in the call asked.

“What's in the name? officer when the information is important.” He replied and continued.

“He's at eleven park hotels in Juhi, Mumbai,” Tatva said.

He disconnected the call.

“And that's it, they can't trace back the call as it's a non-traceable mobile,” Tatva said smashing the mobile by throwing it on the floor.

“What now?” Kala asked.

“Let's wait for another call, let's wait near my landline,” Tatva replied.

A few minutes later:

Tatva's landline phone rang, he picked up the call.

“Hello Ayukta, any update?” Tatva asked.

“Sir, your mobile was switched off.. any problem?”

“It's a long story, what's happening over there? Is there any change?”

Yes sir, officers just left from the location, but there's still a guard outside the hotel's room” he replied.

“Leave that to us,” Tatva said.

CHAPTER NINE

CHAPTER NAVA

Present, SSB Headquarters:

"Did you see Avinashya?" Mahesh asks everyone while he wanders on the aisle searching for her.

He is a 6.2 white complexion man with a muscular body. He was wearing a t-shirt that displays the muscle cuts on his body and a pair of jeans.

As he is passing through the doors on the aisle, he heard sounds coming out of the gym room.

He knocked on the door gently and half-opened it to see what Avinashya was doing.

He was awestruck to see her in action.

Air reflects her as she moves at such speeds, the knives are her are as active as she is. Air screams with pain if it has any kind of life as she rotates and waves her knives utter fast. Her speed is like thunder which strikes first and then makes the sound.

Within a fraction of a second, as Mahesh blinked she started releasing her energy in the form of a giant circle that covers her as she moves fast.

Her hair spread out like an angry lion that nods its head and spreads its mane.

As part of practice, she turned over and noticed Mahesh standing at the door with his eyes wide open and sweating.

She stopped her practice and finally Mahesh gets a glimpse of her looks when she is angry.

He gulped in fear to look at the fearsome face of hers with eyes that turned red and hair standing still up in the air for a few seconds even after she stopped.

Her dress was torn with sharp slices of air that reflected from the walls of the room as she waved her knives.

Her sharp corner teeth, going slowly back in.

"Hi baby, I didn't see you there!" Avinashya said.

"I... um... I have something to tell you, why don't we go somewhere and talk?" Mahesh asked.

"Sure," Avinashya replied.

She took her jacket from the locker and wore it on her tank top.

As they were walking on the aisle Mahesh started talking.

They sat in her car.

"Avinashya, I am not Mahesh.." he continued.

19 years earlier, hotel where Vulcan was hiding, somewhere in India:

Prayogya and Tatva in their human forms of Devansh and Marthand knocked on the window glass of the driver's door where Ayukta was sitting.

Ayukta rolled down the window.

"I guess you're Ayukta, Kundan asked us a favour. I am Marthand Raj, central home minister" Tatva in the form of Marthand said.

"I know you, sir, nice to meet you, I am Ayukta"

"Ok, this is what we will do.. my self and army chief Devansh will go in, talk to him, get him without any force applied, make him sit in your car" Marthand continued.

"You take him to this address," he said while handing over the visiting card with the address written on it.

"What is this place sir? Is it safe?" Ayukta asked.

"It's my guest house.. show this card to the guards outside and they will let you in."

"Okay sir"

"Right! Now wait for us to fetch this guy".

Marthand and Devansh started walking towards the entrance of the hotel.

The guard waiting outside stood up from his chair and saluted him as they walk into the hotel.

"Vulcan" what's his room number? Devansh asked the receptionist.

"There's no one with such name here sir" he replied.

"Guard, come in once" Marthand shouted.

Guard heard it and came running into the hotel towards the reception.

He saluted again and said "Sir".

"What's your name?" Marthand asked.

"Venkat, sir"

"Venkat, you're doing a very good job, you must be rewarded," Marthand said tapping his shoulder.

"Thank you, sir"

"Well, what's our intel on this guy Vulcan? What's his room number is?"

"Sir, I don't know if I am allowed to do that sir, it's confidential"

"Yeah, I know I know, I am just testing if you have all the details, you know, validating you for your promotion"

"Promotion? Sir, it's 208, the second floor, to the right, we suspect that he is living here by the name James David"

"Great!! Venkat, what's your full name?"

"Venkat Rao"

"Well, Nice to meet you, Venkat, I will make sure you will get your promotion letter by tomorrow, good luck"

Guard left as Marthand and Devansh started going to the second floor.

They arrived at 208, Prayogya in the form of army chief Devansh knocked on the door. They've got a visual confirmation.

It was Vulcan in his foul-smelling room, writing in some notebook.

"Now" Marthand shouted.

Prayogya touched Vulcan's face with his hand, which left him hypnotized and agreeing to do whatever they are asking him to do.

They walked him down through the steps holding him.

"Go and manage the guard," Devansh said.

Marthand went to the door and started making conversation with the guard while Devansh started walking him again towards the car while the guard wasn't looking.

"Take him to the guest house, we'll be there as soon as possible.." Devansh said while making Vulcan sit in the car.

Devansh closed the door and Ayukta drove the car and left the place.

Devansh walked back towards Marthand, who was talking to the guard.

"Let's go Marthand," Devansh said.

Marthand dragged Devansh holding his arm away from the guard and started whispering.

"The guard says, Vulcan has a book with a formula written in it...the way to create the virus. We must have this guy killed and retrieve the book before we do that" Marthand said.

"Fine, none of that's going to happen if we stand here whispering to each other, let's move" Devansh replied whispering.

❧❧❧

Same time, Marthand's guest house, somewhere in India:

"Do you think they will let us in?" Devansh asked Marthand while they both were waiting outside the guest house in 70 meters distance.

"They have to, it's Marthand's guest house, I think they will see me and recognize me"

"Oh, you think?"

"Why are you worrying? It seems like Ayukta already went in, as his car isn't outside. If they let us in, well and good, if not use your hypnotism trick"

"You would like it.. wouldn't you? It's not humans' hypnotism, it's the divine's trick called "Nischala", which means without any movement." Devansh said.

"Why to bother explaining to you, you seem to like human methods more, yeah, it's hypnotism and I cannot do it very often as it will have adverse effects," Devansh said.

"Like what?"

"Well, not on angels, but humans, multiple hypnotism may lead to death, so I cannot hypnotize the one I already did, and the state will wear off very soon if I keep doing it in the same day"

"You mean, if you hypnotize guard, he will come out of it very soon and will be aware of us being in the house"

"Exactly"

"Well, thanks for telling me though, I kind of made up my mind that your hypnosis will be plan B if Vulcan doesn't open his mouth, now that's not an option," Marthand said.

He started the car and drove to the gate of the house.

A guard, one among the four, noticed Marthand in the car and commanded to open the door. As the door opened

Marthand drove the car into the parking area.

"See, walk in the park, that's how easy it is," Marthand said while getting out of the car.

Ayukta waiting outside at the door received them.

Vulcan was beaten up and tied to his chair.

"Go ahead and kill me, you will never get your hands on my formula," Vulcan said in a Russian accent.

"Oh, trust me, you will" Marthand said.

He took out his mobile and called someone.

"Kill his daughter," Marthand said to the guy on the phone.

"Don't you dare touch my daughter?" Vulcan said by forcing himself to get up from the chair.

"Vulcan, look at your daughter, remind her one last time before she's dead. You have two options in front of you. You either give up the recipe and live, or you'll die, your daughter dies and your wife dies" Marthand said showing Vulcan his phone.

"Please don't kill her, promise me," Vulcan asked crying.

"You have my word," Devansh said.

"Locker # 202, Bank of Business, 3rd Avenue, Moscow. The passcode is 191812221114" Vulcan said.

"Confirm me if you find it," Marthand said to the guy who's been online on the phone and disconnected the call.

After a few minutes, Marthand's mobile rang and he lifted the call and put it on speaker.

"There's a book here," he said.

"Kill him," said Marthand to the goon.

Devansh and Marthand walked out of the bedroom.

A few moments later:

Marthand and Devansh came back and found Ayukta lying down and the ropes on the chair untied.

"What happened here?" Devansh asked.

"Sir, someone from behind hit me and released Vulcan before I kill him," Ayukta said.

"Well, isn't it great!" Marthand said.

"Sir, we do have what we need. Didn't we?" Ayukta asked.

"No, it turned out that my man in Russia had this book reviewed by some other biologist. It's a PhD. Thesis, he said, we are fooled. We don't have Vulcan and we don't have the formula" Marthand said.

"Is your person in Russia trustworthy?" Devansh asked.

"I cannot believe you're asking me this, I already told you" Marthand dragged Devansh into the living room, closed the bedroom door.

"I lived on earth since the evolution of humans, so when I tell you I know someone in Russia, then you must believe that I have a fucking follower in Russia too" Marthand replied angrily.

"Cool down, we can find him. Open the book and see where he is now"

Marthand raised his hand as the book of existence appeared in the form of sprinkles.

He placed the book on the coffee table, placed one hand on the left side of his chest and rotated his other around the book.

Book automatically opened up a page exposing his location.

"Where is he?" Devansh asked.

"It wouldn't matter, we cannot go there?"

"What do you mean? We can go anywhere.. where is it?"

"It's Subash's house. He is a journalist. This is how it starts, the creator of apocalypse and the designer of apocalypse met each other." Marthand said in intense.

"He will be the red priest who will lead a cult and start this apocalypse." He said.

CHAPTER TEN

CHAPTER DASHA

Same time, At the hospital, somewhere in India:

Devansh, Marthand and Kala in human form walked into the hospital and found Vulcan, Subash and Indhu waiting at the reception queue.

"It's pain in the... well, forget it. We gave him one job, to guard Vulcan, he failed at that and in addition, we had to get him to the hospital for his injuries. This only keeps getting better" Devansh said sarcastically.

As soon as they saw them, they hid behind the wall.

"What do we do now?" Devansh asked.

"Let's lose Ayukta, he can manage a little pain for some time, I have a plan," Kala said and continued.

"I see that Subhash's wife is pregnant, I need a pregnant woman to inject my blood into. I think I can transform myself as a doctor and do it"

"How are they going to visit you. They might have a doctor already." Devansh said.

As he finished saying that, Marthand and Kala looked at him.

"Common, give me a break, why don't you guys learn the trick. I did it once today, I don't know if it will hold the receptionist for long!"

"We don't need long; we just need her to send them to my room," Kala said.

"Alright!! Here goes" Devansh said and lifted his hand directing towards the receptionist.

"We are here for our regular checkup with Dr. Sushree," Subhash said to the receptionist.

"I'm sorry, Dr. Sushree has passed away in a car accident yesterday. We have Dr. Sathish replace her. I can arrange a meeting with him if you like!" The receptionist repeated while Devansh said the exact words hiding.

"I'm sorry to hear it, we are good to meet Dr. Sathish. Thank you" said Subhash.

Indhu and Subhash were sent to Dr. Sathish while Vulcan was waiting in the common waiting area.

Kala transformed himself and started walking very fast to find an empty room.

As he was walking faster, he realized himself.

"Wait a minute, injecting my blood into an adult will kill her, that would make a killer which may end up me burning eternally or burnt into ashes by mother. What should I do!?"

As he was thinking, he hit a nurse.

"Sorry," he said and started walking. He then realized one more thing.

"Come with me," Kala said to the Nurse

They both walked into the sonogram room.

As soon as they entered Subhash and Indhu came in.

"Hello Dr. Sathish, we are here for our regular checkup," Subhash said.

"Nurse, take their sonogram and get me the reports," Kala said.

"Sure doctor."

Subash and Indhu went into the sonogram room.

Kala sat outside in his room, took out a syringe, pushed it into his body and started pulling out his blood.

The blood in the syringe was dark red with little spots of power cells in it.

Syringe heated up with the power cells contained in it.

"I must inject it before the container's physical appearance changes," Kala thought of himself.

Kala stood up, knocked on the sonogram room and opened it halfway.

"Nurse, can you come here for a minute?" Kala asked Nurse through the door.

The nurse walked out closing the door on his way out.

"Give this injection to the mother, it contains vitamins for the baby"

"Sure doctor," Nurse said and walked back into the room.

The nurse tried injecting her the blood.

"Wait, what is it for?" Subash asked.

"It's vitamins for the mother and the baby" the nurse replied.

The nurse injected her with the blood of the divine. As soon as he injected it, the veins on her body started showing signs of divine power by exposing little sparks in her bloodstream.

Indhu felt the pain throughout her body as the power cells started replacing her blood with the divine's blood.

The reaction in her body started stopping the baby from getting any oxygen through the mother.

He took the sonogram reports and walked back to the doctor.

"Doctor, can I talk to you?" the nurse asked.

"Doctor, the baby is not showing any signs of a heartbeat!" the nurse said to Sathish.

"Ok send them in," Kala said in the form of Sathish.

"Mr&Mrs. Subhash, I'm afraid I have bad news," Sathish said in a sad tone.

Subhash and Indhu started holding hands.

"What is it, doctor? Is the baby fine?" Indhu asked.

"Well, it's about that, the baby is showing no signs of heartbeat, in other words, the baby isn't alive." He said.

Indhu started crying after hearing the news. Subhash put his hand around his wife and started soothing her.

"It's ok Indhu," he said.

"We have to remove the baby's body; else it will be a problem for the mother," Sathish said.

"Mrs. Indhu, I would like to talk to you alone before you accept this procedure." He said.

"The baby was completely healthy, but I injected a poison that will kill the baby," Kala said.

"What do you mean?"

"Indhu, you do not have much time, please listen to me carefully, we have to perform surgery and get the baby out, and also I assure you that I will bring the baby back to life. I will ensure that baby is taken good care of."

"Why are you telling me all this?"

"Because you will die in a couple of hours."

"What do you mean I'll die in a couple of hours? Is this some kind of a sick joke? What's happening here?" Indhu asked with anger and annoyance in her voice.

"Subash??" She started shouting.

Her voice wasn't loud enough to leave the doctor's room.

She tried shouting again, but the sound wouldn't come out.

Her throat started turning red with veins popping out in red colour.

"It's happening earlier than I expected, I am sorry Mrs. Subash, I assure you'll reach heaven for the sacrifice that you are doing today for the sake of this world, and mankind," Kala said in his human form as a doctor.

Blood in her body started rejecting the divine's blood. Every little nerve and veins started turning red by popping out on her skin of hers which were visible. As the time passed by second, it started becoming much more severe.

Pores on the skin started bleeding.

"You must not die in pain; I summon the angel of Realms Reacher Tatva and Messenger of the King himself Prayogya at this instant," Kala said out loud to himself.

The equipment in the doctor's room started vibrating vigorously as they both presented themselves from the reception lobby to the doctor's room.

Prayogya touched her with his palm, bringing her into trans. Indhu sat still looking at Kala while the blood completely bled out.

"Mr. Subash must be waiting outside; we must operate her and bring the baby out." He said.

Prayogya cut open the womb and was surprised to see a giant red ball protecting the baby inside the womb. He extended his hand and touched the red ball to bring the baby out.

Three of them stood in circles and held each other's hands, they started chanting a mantra themselves creating a red tornado whooshing in between the circle.

They left the hands and directed the tornado with their hands towards the red ball.

As soon as the tornado touched the red ball, it broke into the baby's body in the form of air.

The baby woke up, started crying as Tatva took her in his hands.

"What now?" He asked.

"We have two tasks. One is to protect the baby till she is 20 years old, and the other is to get rid of Indhu's body." Said Prayogya.

"I think, I have a plan" replied Kala.

"Subash is expecting his wife to return from the operation, we cannot bring her back to life. It's unauthorized and against nature's will." Kala replied.

"But didn't we just bring this little girl back to life?" Tatva asked.

"She wasn't even had a life to start with. She was just born and didn't even open her eyes to see the world. I knew that we are making mistakes after mistakes. But bringing this little one back to life isn't a mistake. But an adult who died as part of the process would be" Kala replied and continued.

"We've come a long way. There's no going back" Kala said and vanished into ashes.

CHAPTER ELEVEN

CHAPTER EKAADASHA

Present, somewhere in India:

"What do you mean you're not Mahesh?" Avinashya said to Mahesh with her head turned back towards the back seat of her car.

"Your mother, Indhu, did a huge sacrifice for the sake of mankind. She didn't get to choose, and there isn't a day that goes by without me regretting what happened to her." He continued.

"She was a beautiful woman, who wanted to have a child in her life fulfilling her dream family, which she didn't get to have in the end."

"All we can ensure was to make sure that she went to heaven. I know it isn't enough for the mistake that we did. But it's for the greater deeds. When it comes to sacrificing one soul to save trillions of humans, it felt right at that time."

"How do you know about my mother?" She asked wiping her tears.

"I was there Avinashya"

"No, it's not possible, if she died 20 years ago, then you might not even be born"

“As I said, I am not Mahesh.”

“Then who the fuck are you?” She shouted in anger and annoyance.

“Messenger and brother of the king of angels, Kala. Only one who can wield the mightiest of swords ‘The Soul Taker’. I am Prayogya and I have been here as your guardian” Mahesh said.

“Dude, pro what? You don’t even make sense!”

Mahesh turned himself into his divine form slowly. The jacket on him turned into the glowing shield. A crown presented itself on his head glowing with jewels in it. A mighty sword appeared on his back along with an axe that’s crossed against the sword.

He grew taller as the top of the car started having dents and the suspension of the car went completely down.

Avinashya sat there awestruck looking at him with her mouth open.

He sat there bending himself as the car couldn’t fit his height.

“It’s all true then! Did you kill my mother? Why did you come back as Mahesh? Who was the one that pretended to be my mother while I grew up? What are you? Who is my father?” She asked in wonder.

Present, somewhere in the FOREST:

“A whole new generation, that’s pretty exciting. Vulcan my friend, why don’t you start your manufacturing process for the virus. It’s almost time anyways.” The Red Priest said laughing loudly while the followers were cheering.

The red priest removed his skull mask revealing his identity

“Subash, can I speak with you in private?” Vulcan asked.

The dungeon became silent for a moment, followers started whispering to each other.

Red Priest looked at the followers and shouted "Silence".

He walked towards Vulcan, extended his hand and held him by his shirt collar.

"I go by the name 'The Red Priest'. You better call me that next time" he said in anger.

"Forgive me, my lord. May I speak with you in private please?"

"If it's about your participation in the Great War, then I think there's nothing to speak."

"But I don't want to. I knew that someone killed your wife. But that's not the way of getting revenge."

"You know how my wife was killed? They made me think that she was killed due to my line of work. But I didn't know the truth until I met my guardian angel."

"What? who is it?"

"King of angels, he calls himself. He injected a blood sample into my wife's bloodstream and that killed my wife. It's not even a peaceful death Vulcan, I didn't get to see my wife for the last time. Maaya, the angel of lies and deception showed me how brutal it was. No one should go through this hell Vulcan."

"She showed me the path to avenge my wife's and my kid's death. A path that destroys both the bad as well as Kala's will to stop it. Additionally, he will get to suffer losing his daughter, once I kill Avinashya." She said with rage in his voice.

"I know but why wage this dangerous virus out in the world on those who are innocent and have nothing to do with your wife"

"Don't you get it, my friend! It's the world now... it's filled with people who are irresponsible, who don't follow any rules, who murder each other. There are no innocent people left Vulcan"

"It's not true, we will kill kids who have no idea about this society"

"They will grow up like the rest of the society Vulcan... it's a reset button to the bad in the society"

"No... I have a bad feeling about this. I can't do it"

"My friend" Red Priest raises his hand and places it on Vulcan's shoulder.

He bent a little towards Vulcan's ear and started whispering.

"Do you think you have a choice? I got ready to have my daughter Avinashya killed for this mission... do you think I will spare you and your family?"

"Please, it's unfair, I gave you the book that has steps of preparation. Why do you need me? Any virologist can create it. I just wanted out"

"There's no going out" The Red Priest shouted by looking at the followers and spreading his arms.

"In this war, everyone dies... it's for the new world and goodness that we are going to create from scratch"

He turned his head towards Vulcan.

"You better go and start your process; I don't want your death to happen any sooner," Red Priest said.

Vulcan sighed and walked towards a small opening with the staircase which lead to an aisle with rooms on either side.

He walked into his room, bent and pulled out his luggage backpack under his bed. He placed it on his bed and unzipped it.

He took out an album with a portrait of his family on the album cover.

He opened the album and started looking at the portrait of his daughter.

❧❧❧

19 years earlier, Subash was waiting for the operation to get finished in the hospital:

"Prayogya, Subash is expecting his wife to return. Remember you are a woman who lost her baby... when the time comes, you will be released from this act" Kala said.

As he finished saying that, Prayogya transformed himself into Indhu and laid on the operation bed.

"This baby here is our hope for the future. She needs her mother to learn about her powers. She will be under the protection of Tatva." Kala said.

As he finished saying that, Tatva held the baby and transformed himself into Indhu who is her birth mother.

"Why did you transform into Indhu?" Prayogya asked lying on the bed.

"The baby deserves to know how her mother looks. We are responsible that she doesn't have a mother anymore. The least I could do is to make sure to pretend as her" He replied.

"Prayogya and Tatva, our jobs are certain now. Prayogya, you pretend to be the wife of Subash who just lost their baby. And Tatva you pretend to be the mother of this child who has no father" Kala said.

"Why can't I simply take the baby with me and take care of her?" Prayogya asked.

"Subhash thinks that the baby is dead, and we are responsible that his wife is no more. He cannot know about the baby. Baby should grow in an environment where she can learn about her powers. Living with humans and around them may not help our mission." Kala said and continued.

"The baby should be isolated from the rest of the world till she learns about her powers. We cannot do it if you take the baby with you" he said looking at Prayogya lying on the bed.

"Wait for my call... Tatva you may leave now" he said.

CHAPTER TWELVE

CHAPTER DVAADASHA

17 years earlier, somewhere in India:

"Indhu, I am going to the office," Subash said to Prayogya in the form of Indhu as he walked towards the door.

Indhu came behind him and stood.

"Okay" she replied standing behind him at the door.

He turned back and held Indhu's face in his hands.

"Indhu, I lost something as much as you did, but it's been two years and we have to move on"

"I've moved on, I am fine"

"No, you are not... you hardly ever talk to me, we haven't even touched each other's hands since the baby died. Do you think it's my fault?"

"You've asked this question multiple times Subash, and no, it's not your fault. It's just hard for me to get back to normal"

"I understand"

"No, you don't, if you do, you will let me be"

"How can I let you be? You are my wife, I love you. It kills me to see you like this."

“I cannot have this same conversation again and again Subash, I have work to do,” she said and left into the kitchen.

Indhu walked into the kitchen and saw Subash leaving in his car from the kitchen’s window.

As Subhash’s car left the road, the lights in the house started blinking. The tables started vibrating vigorously making the things on the table fell off.

Indhu ran out into the living room to a sight of things vibrating as if there was an earthquake.

A beam of light suddenly appeared in the center of the living room making a huge buzzing sound.

“It’s time finally” Indhu shouted in the voice of Prayogya loudly spreading her arms.

The light beam cleared to which Kala presented himself in his divine form, wearing a white glowing shield with a crown.

“Your highness” Indhu kneeled in front of Kala.

“Raise brother, it’s time,” Kala said.

“What about Subash?”

“I’ve made a plan”

He transformed himself into a normal human taking a different Russian mob gangster’s face wearing a black leather jacket.

He picked up the landline receiver.

“Tell Subhash’s number,” he asked and started dialling.

“Hey Indhu, any issue?” Subash asked on the phone noticing the home number.

“This is Duncan speaking. I know you have Vulcan with you. Hand him over, else your wife will die a gruesome death” Kala said and disconnected the call.

“What are you doing brother?” Prayogya asked.

"Vulcan is not with Subash, he is hiding in Subash's cousin's guest house at Chennai"

"So, what are you planning to do?"

"Sit on this chair," Kala said dragging a chair to the center of the living room.

Prayogya in the form of Indhu walked towards the chair and sat on it.

As Kala waved his hand, a roped appeared in his palm.

He tied Indhu to the chair. He walked towards the kitchen and got a meat knife.

"I got your plan brother," Prayogya said.

"Act along"

"I will, but aren't we pushing his limits? He lost his child, he lost his happiness as I who am his wife doesn't let him touch if he sees his wife dying in front of him, that will break him into pieces"

"We all lost something in this war, didn't we Brother?, I, the king of angels broke most of the mother's rules. Who knows what may happen to me when mother awakes!? I want to make sure that I finish everything that I started"

"Brother, I am not sure how successful we will be, but the pain we are causing to these people is unforgivable"

"I know brother, remember how a war killed thousands of soldiers because one person dreamed of seeing his country in great power.. it's a much greater deed than that".

As he finished saying that, a car came and stopped by at very fast speeds in front of the door.

Subash opened the car door and got out of his car. He ran towards the house entrance with panic.

He ran into the house to the view of Kala holding the knife on the throat of Indhu.

"You failed to do the one thing that I asked you," Kala said in the form of Duncan.

"He is not with me, please... I made the call, he is on his way, trust me" he said begging.

"Trust?? That's the hardest thing you can expect from me.. you leave me no other option than to kill her"

As he finished saying that, Subash jumped over the chair and grabbed the knife and attacked Kala.

Kala looked at the sharp edge of the knife controlling it telekinetically as Subash tried stabbing him. His hand wouldn't go any nearer to his body.

He tried stabbing again by applying more pressure.

Kala held the hand of Subash who was holding the knife.

"It's not your wife who is supposed to be tied up. It's you" Kala said as he slightly touched Subash on his face.

The divine power of Kala is no match to any human, resulting in Subash fleeing over and hitting the TV which was at the entertainment unit.

He wasn't able to move as he hurt his spine.

Kala dragged another chair, lifted Subash and made him sit on the chair. He untied Indhu and used the same ropes to tie Subash.

He picked up the knife that fell on the floor.

"Now I am sure that Vulcan isn't coming." He said and pretended as if he slit the throat of Indhu.

Prayogya who is in the form of Indhu started bleeding, she has fallen on the floor extending her hand towards Subash, crying.

"Take care of yourself Subash," she said and closed her eyes slowly.

Kala dragged her through the living room in front of Subash's eyes, lifted her, made her sit in the car of Subash and drove away.

He sat there on the chair crying with his hands and legs tied to the chair helplessly.

"I know you think it's your fault that our child was dead, but it's not Indhu. That's what I wanted to tell you"

"Your death will not go in vain. I will find Duncan and avenge your death" he said weeping.

14 years earlier, somewhere in India:

"Avinashya, wake up, it's time for your practice," said Saavi who is Tatva in the form of Indhu.

"Mom, just a few more minutes," Avinashya said in her sleepy voice pulling up her sheets towards her face.

"I was living a royal life just before all this, how did I wind up in this mother and daughter drama" Saavi thought to herself.

"Avinashya, you either get up now, or you'll get punishment," she said angrily.

Avinashya sat up suddenly from the bed.

"No mom, this is not fair," she said hitting her hands on the bed with a disappointed tone.

"Go, brush your teeth and come out into the garden," Saavi said and walked out of her bedroom.

Saavi walked into the garden which was like a military training campsite. The house was a big mansion that consists of a thin protective untouchable and non-penetrate film surrounding the house, which hides it from the real world and is located in the middle of the forests

From inside the film, the world on the outside looks as it is, only that the one on the inside can see the things on the outside.

Avinashya walked out wearing her pyjamas. She walked into the garden and spread her hand wide and started breathing the fresh air.

"Avinashya let's make use of the morning light... come on, time to train" Saavi shouted so that Avinashya can hear.

Avinashya started her training. She laid on the ground upside down with her legs and arms spread wide to do push-ups.

"Mom, why am I not allowed to go outside" with a cute voice.

Saavi looked at her with a sad face.

"I know honey, no one should deserve this. But you are special sweetie... you know that mother is just protecting you from the real world.. don't you?" She said holding Avinashya's face.

"Mom?"

"Yes, honey?"

"What are you protecting me from?"

"Wish I could tell you, sweetie... it's just not the time yet."

"But I am ready, I am learning this since I am 3 years old."

"It's not about being ready baby, it's about knowing how special you are... and when you do... there's no turning back"

"Mom, can I at least go to school?"

"School? You are getting all the education you need here! Why do you need a school?"

"Mom, you said yourself, that no one deserves this. I want to go to school, make friends... please mom"

"Sorry honey... that I cannot allow, you know that right!"

"Mom, please, mom"

"Avinashya, I said no..." she replied in an angry tone.

Avinashya stood up and ran into the house crying.

Saavi sighed in frustration holding her forehead with her palm.

"Honey, I am sorry that I shouted at you... but I think you are old enough to understand, the precision, the accuracy and the speed you have aren't normal.. hope you recognize that" she continued.

"World out there is dangerous, people like you are not safe."

Saavi looked down and took a couple of seconds to think.

"Okay! Here's the deal... I take you outside to a mall for shopping. You don't get to have this conversation again ever"

Avinashya walked out wearing a white shirt with a black jacket along with trousers and so did Saavi.

She unlocked the car, they both sat in, she chanted something in her mouth, the thin film started to separate creating a wide opening in the form of a door opening sideways.

"Whoa! That's cool! I have never seen it.. how did you unlock it, mom?"

"You shouldn't know it!"

"Why?"

"You know why!"

She drove the car outside the film which closed itself again and sealed from both inside and outside.

"Mom, how is it?" Avinashya asked Saavi showing a gown in a clothing shop

"It's a prom dress Avinashya, you are neither old nor going to school to have that"

"At least I can try it on.. right!"

"Sure, why not?"

Avinashya removed the dress from the display, she took it to the fitting rooms to try it on.

“Hi, I am looking for pants for a kid of 10 years old,” someone said to the representative standing near the kid’s section dresses behind Saavi.

“I heard this voice earlier” Saavi thought and turned back.

She was shocked to see Subash standing there talking with the representative.

“Oh my god! What should I do now?” She stood there facing him thinking.

“What’s the kid’s height sir?” The representative asked.

“Well, I am not sure, he is the son of my boss... it’s his birthday so..” Subash replied

He was looking around to find if any pant height would match the kid’s height.

“Indhu?” He shouted in surprise seeing Saavi in the form of over there.

Saavi turned back and started walking fast between the aisle trying to hide from him.

“Indhu? Indhu..” he started shouting much louder.

He noticed her walking away fast.

“Excuse me,” he said to the representative and started following her.

She walked out of the shop into the common area and started running.

“Indhu... stop” he started running behind her shouting.

“Oh, what should I do! What should I do!” Saavi thought running faster.

She ran out of the mall onto the road and vanished into sprinkles whereas Subash was slowed down.

Subash walked out on the road.

“Indhu?” He started searching the nearby roads.

“Mom? How does it look?” Avinashya came out of the fitting rooms and asked.

"Mom? Mom?" She started shouting as she couldn't find her mother.

16 years earlier, somewhere in another realm:

Saavi escaped into sparkles and presented herself in the throne room in front of Kala.

He was sitting on the throne closing his eyes and watching over the realms. Hydra, the giant three-headed serpent which was guarding the door of the forbidden room, behind the throne of Kala, where the mother was sleeping, hissed as Saavi presented herself in the throne room.

"Hello to you too, sister.. hope you are well," Saavi said as she transformed herself into Tatva, the angel for realm reachers.

He grew as tall as the rest of the angels who are 14ft in height, he transformed his attire into a white long dress with a red scarf around his neck and a goatee beard.

He looked at his left arm and wondered to see the book of existence missing as he transformed himself.

Kala opened his eyes by hearing the voice of Tatva.

"What's the reason for your sudden visit? How's Avinashya?" He asked.

"I think you knew it already, what were you doing closing your eyes? Sleeping? Aren't you monitoring the realms"?

"Yes, but I want to hear the foolish thing that you did from your mouth"

"It's not a big deal, I can go back again... I left Avinashya in the mall... I can go back to her if I can place where she is"

"Then what's late? Use your book and go back"

"I can go back, but I lost the book"

"What do you mean you lost the book?"

"When I created the hideout mansion of Avinashya, I didn't want her to see the book lying around in the house. So, I changed it to the bracelet and was wearing it to my hand"

"And?"

"And I think I lost the bracelet"

"How could you do that? You know how important that book is for the source of your powers?"

"It's fine, no human can turn it back.."

"Alright! Let's think of an alternative way"

"How can we find Avinashya"

"We cannot place her... unless she uses her powers."

"What do you mean"

"Once she uses powers, we can see the power of supernatural being on earth"

"You're the angel of realms.. you can identify people right?"

"Yes, but she is not people.. so, the laws of mortals don't apply to her.."

"So, we wait then, you go back to your old Kundan form and try searching for her...I will inform you if I find her" Kala said.

CHAPTER THIRTEEN

CHAPTER TRAYODASHA

Present, somewhere in India, house of Avinashya:

"How could you do this to me? I trusted you! I believed you... I thought you're my only family left after my mother left me in the shopping mall" Avinashya said angrily walking into her house.

Her house is a mess filled with clothes lying around on the couch and unwashed utensils in the sink.

A fan that makes a creaking sound as it rotates, leaking from the bathroom tap, paint falling off from the ceiling.

"Is this where you live? Thanks to you... you never invited me into your house!" Prayogya in the form of Mahesh said sarcastically.

"Don't even start with your sarcasm, I am so not in the mood, apparently kids who were left by their moms do not have much money to start with"

"You're mistaken"

"No, no, don't interrupt me... I completely forgot.. she is not even my mother.. some angel who took the form of my mother, changed his name to cheat me, and then betray me by leaving me in some mall like a stray dog."

"We searched everywhere for you Avinashya, we couldn't find you as we lost the book of existence"

"Book of Existence?"

"Yes, we can search for anyone in that book, but Tatva lost it"

"Great!! More divine things that were lost along with me"

"No, you don't understand..."

"No, it's not me who doesn't understand... it's you guys.. have you ever wondered how life would be for a 4-year girl to live on the streets? I was taken into foster care and guess what? They made me their slave.. that's not even the worst part.. they tortured me, they hit me, I haven't had any education if it wasn't for Subash"

"He is not the good person"

"What do you mean? he's my father."

"No, he is not. Kala, king of gods is your father. He is the Red Priest."

"That's some bullshit. My father can't be the Red Priest"

"I saw it, I know it. His depression and his vulnerability made him start a cult. His cult main goal is to wipe out the insects on this rock which are humans." Prayogya continued.

"The virus he found is deadly and can wipe out every human on this planet."

"Then why don't you angels stop it?"

"We can't, our brother Mruthyu shed a light on us. We were misdirected by our sister Maaya. She created an illusion of apocalypse in Kala's head, she injected an idea of having a child with a human can save this planet.

But the actions that Kala, myself and Tatva did for that are unforgivable. We were the reason your mother was dead; we were the reason you didn't have a proper life.

Having lost his wife and his child, he started a cult. And Maaya powers them under the greed of becoming an almighty.

The mistake had been done, kid. We angels cannot fight among ourselves even if we want to because of Mother's rule that restrains us.

So, you are our only option against her.

"Well, guess what? Tables have turned.. he grew me up, he gave me life, I am what I am right now because of him.. after all, he is trying to create a better world"

"By killing trillions of people?"

"Well, at least he is doing that!! What are you doing? Losing books, leaving kids on roads, murdering parents, threatening powerless creatures, playing with an individual's feelings? Aren't you guys are supposed to get rid of the misery in this world? I believe you're just creating more misery"

"It's not how it works Avinashya.. world might be earth to you... but this universe is vast... there are laws.. humans aren't part of the plan, but when you creatures came into existence, mother had to develop new laws so that we will not mess with your lives"

"And here you are doing exactly opposite of that"

"Yes, we destroyed lives, we are the reason for deaths, we threatened people, but it's for the greater goods"

"You know what! Write a card and hang it over your neck.. because you should tell that yourself till you die... it will save some time at least"

"Avinashya, cool down.. listen to me.. when humans are created there's nothing but happiness because of their innocent lives.. they kill, eat and sleep.. but Sarga designed humans just like us, their brains can think and evolve.. they are angels without any powers... when those brains started thinking they invented things... they invented money to buy things... it's all where the misery was started"

"I couldn't care less for this bullshit... I had been betrayed by you guys... I might as well go and team up with my father" the electric buzz on the fingers started as she started getting angrier.. it started turning red and her voice started being distorted.

Mahesh looked at her change, he noticed the demonic voice, her sharp teeth coming out of her lips, her eyes turning red slowly.

"Avinashya.. listen to me ... calm down.. when Tatva lost you, we couldn't find you unless you used powers.. when you killed three men when you were 10, that's when we found you...

But it was too late, you went with Subash.. when you grew up and Subash wanted to kill you... I was sent to be with you to protect you all the time... but I don't know, you fell in love with me... and so did I. I never left your side ever since... I made myself a curse that would take me where ever you are when you cry" He continued.

"I am so sorry that it all started with a lie.. but think about all the children who would lose their mothers when they were brought into this world. Goodness in society should be achieved by change within us. Not by killing trillions of innocent people"

"Do you want to support someone who wants to build a new world on the graves of these innocent people? If you do.. then there's nothing I can do to stop you"

"When my brother, your father Kala brought you into this world, he knew that this could cause more destruction or stop it.. he took the risk anyway because of the faith that he had in his bloodline... I am sorry for everything that you went through... I will do it again in a better way if you want... but that doesn't change anything"

"I believe the circumstances made you much stronger and powerful. If you still want to join the cult.. you know where they are... I wouldn't stop you"

Avinashya's teeth started going back in, and her eyes turned back into normal colour.

"Alright! I'll fight... but we are over... I just can't be with a guy who started this relationship with a lie... and not a million older by age of course"

Prayogya and Avinashya laughed hugging.

"Avinashya there's one more thing you should know... you are having the powers of an angel.. unless and until you know about your powers and have peace and calm in you, whenever you get angry, you will lose control over them, you turn yourself into a demonic form"

"How can I control my powers? I don't even know what powers I possess"

"As a daughter of Kala, time doesn't affect you... so, you don't age past 25... you won't die unless killed by an angel or any celestial weapon.. you were fed and given life by Tatva too, the realms reacher.. so, you can be accurate, intelligent, decisive, and fast. Last but not least, when you were given life using the three-star mantra... you have part of me in you... so you are strongest and mightiest... I wouldn't be surprised if you wield the sword of soul takers one day."

"Cool!!! Can you teach me"

"You just have to believe in yourself... you'll know how to use them when the time comes"

CHAPTER FOURTEEN

CHAPTER CHATURDASHA

Present, SSB headquarters, somewhere in India:

"So, are you telling that there were attacks on me even when I was a kid?" Avinashya asked Mahesh walking into the entrance of the SSB headquarters.

"Yes, and it was not the red cult always, sometimes it was your teachers, your neighbours, Maaya and the red cult manipulated the brains of the people around you and attacked you. I was your secret protector, I figured out that I cannot protect you for so long and you have to learn how to protect yourself.. that's when I stopped"

"Thanks for being there for me.." She said looking at him.

Officers started running down on the ground floor out from the cell room in hurry for life. Avinashya stopped one officer.

"What happened?" She asked an officer.

"A demon-like creature just came off from the floor and started breaking walls. It broke the cell of Dior and took him." He said in fear and ran away.

"Demon? Do you know what it is?" Avinashya asked Mahesh.

“There are many of them... but every one of them is in jail... except one” he replied.

“Who? It’s Hades, the strongest and the mightiest among the demons. Only Maaya can summon him.”

Present, dungeons of the Red Priest, in the forest, somewhere in India:

“I think I can handle these mad cults, why do we need a battalion?” Avinashya asked Mahesh getting down from a parked car in the forest with a battalion of commandos following her.

“Father, please come out and surrender yourself along with your cult. It’s over, there’s a battalion out here” she said into the saxophone.

The red priest along with the demon of 14ft tall and the members of the cult came out of the dungeon.

“My god! That’s too many people and it’s one ugly demon” Avinashya said sarcastically and continued.

“Why don’t you take the demon, I will take care of the rest, he is not a human right,” Avinashya asked.

“We are not supposed to. I told you, even if we want, we can’t because of Mother’s restraints on us.”

She closed her eyes and transformed herself into an angelic form. She started flowing with a white shield glowing with glitter and the headband with a half-closed eye on it.

“It’s up to you now, I must go inside and protect Vulcan,” said the red priest and walked back into the dungeon.

Hades came running towards Avinashya whereas Mahesh took the battalion to fight with the rest of the cult.

He started throwing blows on Avinashya using his power from Maaya. Where she blocked them with her hands.

Hades, the demon, punched hard on the shield of Avinashya, creating a ripple effect in the air pushing both Hades and Avinashya back.

Avinashya fell on the ground, trying to get back up, she wasn't able to recover from the mighty blow and get back to her angelic form.

Her headband and her shield started vanishing as she started turning back into her normal form.

She found another blow from Hades coming on her way.

"Mahesh, throw your cane" she shouted.

"It's not a cane, it's.."

"Yes I know, the soul taker... I need a weapon"

"But you cannot wield it!"

"Just throw the fucking sword"

As he threw the cane, it started turning into a 7ft sword in the midair, which fell next to her.

She stood up, grabbed the handle seeing Hades running towards her. She was struggling to lift the sword as its very heavy and longer than her height.

She closed her eyes.

"Control your powers from within" she heard it in her mind Mahesh saying it.

She started lifting the sword a bit, as she did, the headband started reappearing. The shield that almost faded and vanished started reappearing.

She lifted the sword halfway through, as she did, she gained her angelic form back.

She started flowing in the air with her hair flowing and her eyes turned completely white.

She lifted the sword with her both arms, she raised it higher as the buzz started flowing through the sword too. The buzz made a crack on the sword"

Two light beams appeared next to Mahesh, blowing off the air, as the beam cleared, Kala and Tatva presented themselves in human forms as Sathish and Kundan.

"Is it.." Kundan stood there surprised looking at Avinashya wielding the sword.

"Mother? I think so!" Mahesh replied.

"It's not mother, it's something beyond. Your sword was created by Sarga and he made sure no one, not even mother could wield that, it's much more powerful" Sathish said looking at her in surprise with the utmost respect in his voice.

She swung the sword of soul taker, creating a mighty strike of lightning pushing back Hades.

Hades fell to the ground taking the blow from the sword. Avinashya landed on the ground holding the handle with one hand, leaving the sword on the ground.

She dragged the sword on the ground as she walked towards Dior and Hades.

She stood in front of them.

Officers went into the dungeon and attacked Vulcan and the Red priest.

"It's for the betterment of the society" Red Priest started shouting as the officers arrested them both.

A much bolder and hotter fire beam stroke Hades lying on the ground from her another eye on the headband.

"Ahh" they kept shouting in pain shaking their hands.

He turned into ashes, but the beam wouldn't go off.

Kala, Tatva and Prayogya walked towards Avinashya by transforming themselves into the divine form.

They kneeled in front of her as she wouldn't close the eye that emits the beam.

"Please cool down... it's over" Kala said.

Clouds started raging along with the thunders in the sky.

The dust rises covering Avinashya. As the dust cleared, she was holding the mighty flaming sword.

Angels were awestruck to see the image of it.

"I've heard, that none of the angels could wield it as it's Father's spine," said one of the angels.

"I am Singularity, I go by another name. The Father." Avinashya said in a deep voice.

Present, throne room, somewhere in another Realm:

Hydra sleeping on the door of the forbidden room hissing wakes up to the rattle sounds of the door.

Hydra is a 25ft long brown colour three-headed serpent guarding the door where The Mother's sleeping

The door started to vibrate vigorously, Hydra spreads its hood and starts crawling down.

As she crawled down completely, the door bangs open to the view of utter blackness which has nothing but void.

Hydra turns herself into an angelic form with a fire burning over her body.

"Mother!!!" She says in surprise and kneeled.

Two large oval-shaped white eyes open in the void leaving the void brighter.

The mother awakens.

To be continued
In Volume # 2

9 798886 298123

Printed by Libri Plureos GmbH in Hamburg,
Germany